D0369053

ISBN 0-86163-463-2

Copyright © 1990 Award Publications Limited

This edition first published 1990 by
Award Publications Limited,
Spring House, Spring Place,
Kentish Town, London NW5 3BH

Printed in Germany

MR. TOAD

from Kenneth Grahame's
THE WIND IN THE WILLOWS

Adapted by Jane Carruth

Illustrated by Rene Cloke

AWARD PUBLICATIONS

Early one morning in summer Ratty and Mole set about painting and varnishing their boat.

Mole worked as hard as Ratty but he couldn't help wishing they had eaten before they left home.

"I suppose we can go home soon," he said at last. "There's not much to do now."

"Of course we can," said Ratty.

Once home, Ratty set about getting breakfast and they were in the little parlour enjoying their eggs when a heavy knock sounded at the door.

"See who it is, Mole," said Ratty.

Mole ran to the door and opened it. "Goodness, it's you, Mr. Badger," he gasped. "Come in, do!"

Mr. Badger's news soon brought the two friends to their feet. "We'll come at once," Ratty said. "If you want to save that foolish Toad from killing himself in his new car then we will help!"

When they reached Toad Hall, Ratty saw at once that they were just in time. There was Toad, wearing a smart motoring outfit and heavy goggles, about to climb into a powerful new car.

"Grab him!" Badger shouted. "Don't let him get near that car!"

Ratty and Mole obeyed, taking firm hold of the struggling Toad.

As Toad struggled and kicked in an effort to break free, Badger addressed the delivery man. "You may take the car back, my good man," said Badger, in a very lordly manner. "Mr. Toad will not be requiring it after all."

Then, as the car moved away, Badger ordered his friends to take Toad into the house and stay with him.

Toad was spluttering with fury as Ratty and Mole began taking off his motoring clothes.

And then Mr. Badger appeared.

"I'm ashamed of you, Toad," he began in a stern voice. "I've heard that you were boasting that you would be the Terror of the Highway…"

At this Toad struggled more furiously than ever and it took Ratty and Mole all their time to hold him down.

Then, without warning, he lay quite still and said in a feeble voice, "I know I was wrong. Do let me go!"

But no sooner was he on his feet than he shouted, "I'll do what I like — you nosy idiots!"

This was too much for Mr. Badger. He shook Toad quite hard and then led him off to the parlour for a sound talking to.

Ratty and Mole waited anxiously for Badger's return. When he came back at last with Toad he looked very serious.

"Toad is quite impossible," Badger told them. "He refuses to say he is sorry, and he won't give his promise to stay away from fast, powerful cars…"

"No I won't!" Toad shouted.

"Take him away," Badger ordered. "Ratty and Mole take him upstairs and make sure that he doesn't leave his room."

"It's for your own good, Toady," Ratty said, as Toad kicked and struggled all the way to his room. "We'll take turns to watch over you…"

As he was speaking Toad began arranging the bedroom chairs to look like a motor-car. Then he climbed in and began making motor-car noises.

"I'm afraid he really is bad," Ratty whispered. "We'll all just have to stay at Toad Hall and look after him."

Toad paid no attention to his friends. He just went on pretending to be a racing-driver.

After a few days in his room Toad asked Ratty
to come and see him.

"My dear old friend," Toad began in a feeble
whisper, "I am ill. Sleep is impossible and my
poor head throbs…"

"Poor Toady!" Rat murmured.

"Fetch me a doctor from the village," Toad
begged. "It may already be too late but I need
help…"

Now Toad knew that Mole and Badger had gone into the village to get supplies. Ratty and he were alone in Toad Hall!

As soon as Rat had left the room, Toad hopped out of bed. First he tried the door but that was locked. "No matter," he thought, and he knotted the sheets from his bed, making them into a rope.

When this was done to his satisfaction, Toad put on his best suit and filled the pockets with all the money he could find.

By now he was so proud of himself that he broke into a little song.

Then, smiling broadly, he made fast the rope to the centre mullion of the window and began scrambling down as quickly as he could with reckless speed.

When he reached the ground, Toad set off in the opposite direction to the village.

"I expect Ratty is still with the doctor," Toad said to himself, and he began to whistle a merry tune as he hopped and skipped along. "Poor Ratty! Of course he meant well. They all did but how could they imagine the great and mighty Toad would stay a prisoner for long!"

Toad couldn't make up his mind where to go so he just kept on walking.

He stopped at the first little town he came to and marched into the first inn that caught his eye.

By now he was sure that Badger and the others would never catch up with him. He sat down at the table near the door and ordered a very large and expensive meal.

Toad was on his third sausage when the driver of a smart and very expensive motor-car came in and began talking about his car to the innkeeper.

17

Toad took in every word. He stopped feeling hungry. He couldn't finish the sausage for thinking about the car.

At last he got up and went outside to have a look at the motor-car for himself. It was magnificent! It was everything a great car should be!

18

"I wonder if it starts easily?" he asked himself. "I expect it does!"

And before Toad knew what he was doing, he had taken hold of the starting handle and was turning it.

The car started like a dream and at the sound of the engine Toad's eyes gleamed.

In a flash he was in the driving seat, one hand on the wheel, the other on the gear lever and suddenly the car began to move, slowly at first and then it gathered speed.

Poor, foolish Toad! There was only one possible end to his reckless wicked deed! He drove the car so fast and with so little care for other users of the road that soon the traffic police were after him.

Before the morning was over, he was taken prisoner and brought before the magistrate.

"Dear me!" said the magistrate as Toad stood before him under the guard of a watchful policeman, "You have broken the law on several counts…"

"Not guilty!" said Toad in a feeble voice.

"Nonsense!" said the magistrate. "Your crimes cannot be defended. You are guilty and you must go to prison. I sentence you to twenty years."

Toad was then loaded with chains and thrown into the darkest dungeon of an ancient castle which was, at all times, heavily guarded.

As soon as Toad found himself in the dark, horrible dungeon he wept bitter tears. Even the sight of the gaoler's pretty daughter did not raise his spirits.

But as the weeks passed the girl grew fond of Toad and, at last, she thought of a plan to get him out of prison.

One day she brought her aunt, who was a washerwoman, to see him.

By now, of course, the girl knew all about the magnificent Toad Hall. She knew too from the boastful Toad how rich he was. So too did her aunt.

Her plan was simple. One day her aunt would bring some of her oldest washerwoman clothes and an old bonnet. She would help to dress Toad in the clothes and then Toad would pass himself off as the old washerwoman.

Toad agreed at once. And the very next Saturday, the washerwoman came into his cell and proceeded to fit him out in her old clothes.

Mr. Toad awarded the good woman with several gold sovereigns before he left the dungeon.

Clutching his bundle of washing, Toad made his way through the castle. His heart was beating so fast he thought the sentry must hear it. But he kept on and every door and gate was opened for him.

It seemed hours before he heard the big door that led to freedom shut behind him and he sighed with relief. All he could think about was home.

Dizzy with the success of his daring, Toad made for the railway station. Pushing his way to the head of the queue, he asked for a ticket to the nearest village to Toad Hall. But when he groped in the pocket of his rusty old apron for money, he found nothing but an old bent safety-pin!

Horror of horrors! He had left all his money behind…

"No money, no ticket," said the ticket clerk with a nasty sneer.

Black despair filled Toad's heart as he wandered on to the platform and stared up at the huge engine.

"What's the matter, mother?" asked the kindly engine-driver.

"I've l-lost all my money and I c-can't get home," said Toad, and he managed to shed a tear.

After that it was easy to persuade the driver to give him a lift and soon the train was on its way.

All too soon for Toad came the roar of another engine close behind. "They're after me!" he told himself. And when the engine slowed down at a bend, Toad jumped, and rolled down a slope.

Toad went on rolling down the grassy embankment until he managed to stop against a tree. He could hardly believe his good luck as the pursuing engine thundered past.

It was crowded with policemen, warders and soldiers. "And I've outwitted them all," he chuckled, highly pleased with himself. "What a smart fellow I am!"

After he made sure he had no broken bones, Toad made his way deeper into the woods. He was both hungry and tired but the thought of his own cleverness kept him in good heart.

He kept on walking until it grew dark and then, at last, tired out, he found shelter in the hollow of a tree. Soon, he had closed his eyes and was fast asleep.

That night Toad had no bad dreams. Instead he dreamt he was safely back at Toad Hall being given a hero's welcome by all his friends.